Pascal

Based on the million-plus-selling book

BOUNDARIES

by Drs. Henry Cloud and John Townsend

Sophie and Sam

When to Say "Yes" and When to Say "No"

by Tori Cloud • Illustrated by Becky Valentine

INTEGRITY
PUBLISHERS
family
Nashville

Sophie and Sam: When to Say "Yes" and When to Say "No"

Copyright© 2005 by Tori Cloud.

Published in association with Yates & Yates, LLP, Attorneys and Counselors, Orange, California.

Published by Integrity Publishers, a division of Integrity Media, Inc., 5250 Virginia Way, Suite 110, Brentwood, TN 37027

HELPING PEOPLE WORLDWIDE EXPERIENCE the MANIFEST PRESENCE of GOD.

Scripture verses marked CEV® are taken from The Holy Bible, Contemporary English Version®. Copyright© 1995 by American Bible Society.

Verses marked NIV® are taken from The Holy Bible, New International Version®. Copyright© 1973, 1978, 1984 by International Bible Society. Used by permission of Zondervan. All rights reserved.

Verses marked NIrV® are taken from The Holy Bible, New International Reader's Version®. Copyright© 1995, 1996, 1998 by International Bible Society. Used by permission of Zondervan. All rights reserved.

Verses marked NLT® are taken from The Holy Bible, New Living Translation® Copyright © 1996. Used by permission of Tyndale House Publishers, Inc., Wheaton, Illinois 60189. All rights reserved.

Verses marked ICB® are taken from The Holy Bible, International Children's Bible®. Copyright© 1986, 1988 by Word Publishing, a division of Thomas Nelson, Inc.

Library of Congress Cataloging-in-Publication Data [to come]

ISBN: 1-5914-299-6

Printed in Italy

05 06 07 08 PBI 9 8 7 6 5 4 3 2 1

For Olivia and Lucy, with love

With very special thanks to Henry and John,
Laura Minchew and Byron Williamson,
Jeana Ledbetter and Sealy Yates,
and Abi Frederick
for all of your wisdom and support.

DEAR PARENTS:

Welcome to the world of Sophie and Sam! We hope these stories provide many wonderful experiences to laugh and learn together for you and the children you love. We are excited to bring the principles of *Boundaries* to children for the first time.

In 1992, we wrote the book *Boundaries: When to Say "Yes," When to Say "No" to Gain Control of Your Life*. Since then, millions of people have found the *"Boundaries"* principles from God's Word have the power to literally change their lives.

Often, people would say to us, "If I had learned about setting and keeping boundaries as a child, it would have saved me so much pain and heartache! And I don't want my children to have to make the same bad decisions that I did. Can you please write a *Boundaries* book for children?"

A boundary is a property line. It defines where one person ends and another one begins, just like the fence around your house. These stories will illustrate to your children the wonderful things that can happen when they say "yes" to good things and "no" to destructive things. Boundaries will help children in three key areas: moral, personal, and interpersonal relationships.

In childhood, character is developed that will set the tone for future decisions. Children learn lasting character traits each and every day in very simple contexts, like play and friendships. Learning to say "no" to meanies is the same skill that will enable children to avoid getting involved with hurtful people in adolescence and adulthood, when the stakes are much greater. Learning to say "yes" to rules and authority now will make future interactions with bosses and the IRS go much more smoothly! And, most important, learning to be thankful to and walk with God as a child will anchor the rest of life in the most meaningful relationship of all.

The book of Proverbs in the Bible says to instill wisdom above all else. It is our hope that this book can be an important building block in the development of your children, bringing them the safety and joy of living fully in God's boundaries.

God bless,

Henry Cloud, PhD
John Townsend, PhD

TABLE OF CONTENTS

Say Yes to TELLING the TRUTH

The parade was starting very soon!
Sophie and Sam raced into town.
There were floats and music and bright balloons,
But best of all was a sparkly crown.

Sophie squealed, "I want that crown!"
"It doesn't belong to you," Sam said.
But Sophie quickly grabbed the crown
And placed it on her head.

Sam said, "Sophie, put it back!"
"I'm going to," she lied.
But when Sam looked the other way.
She turned and ran to hide.

"Someone stole my sparkly crown!"
A princess cried out from her float.
When Sophie heard that, she got so scared
She hid the crown inside her coat.

"What are you doing by hiding the crown?
Just give it back right now," Sam said.
"But I don't want to get in trouble!" she cried,
Nervously scratching her head.

Just then, a policeman walked up to the pair.
"Did you see who took the crown?"
Sophie and Sam shook their heads "No"
With their eyes staring down at the ground.

The policeman called out, "the parade won't start
'til the princess is wearing her crown.
We need the help of everyone here
To search all around the town."

Sophie and Sam were caught in a lie.
In their hearts, they knew what to do:
God says to always tell the truth
Even if it is hard on you.

Sophie stood up to confess her crime
And felt the crown slipping down her fur.
Clink, clank! It fell to the ground;
Everyone stared straight at her.

"I'm so sorry I didn't tell the truth.
I took the crown and then I lied."
Sophie handed it back to the princess.
"I ruined the parade!" she sighed.

"I forgive you, Sophie," and then with a wink
The princess yelled out, "Let's go! Hooray!"
A marching band of skunks passed by;
The parade was finally underway!

It's important to always speak the truth
With our friends and everyone around.
Because lying doesn't just hurt you;
It could hurt an entire town!

Stop lying and start telling each other the truth.
Ephesians 4:25 CEV

Say Yes to SHARING

There was a mouse named Lola
Who had to have her way.
"It's mine, just mine. I want it all!"
Was her favorite thing to say.

Lola had a birthday party
With cake and gifts galore.
And though she opened all the gifts
She wanted even more.

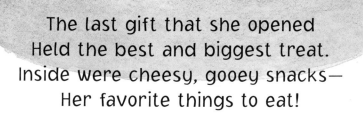

The last gift that she opened
Held the best and biggest treat.
Inside were cheesy, gooey snacks—
Her favorite things to eat!

Her friends asked, "May we have a taste?
We'd love to have some too."
But Lola shoved them in her mouth.
"I will not share with you."

When all her friends got up to play,
Lola stayed to dine.
She didn't share a single treat.
"They're mine, just mine, all mine!"

Lola realized suddenly
That she was feeling icky.
The room was spinning round and round;
Her head felt hot and sticky.

She was stuffed from head to toe,
So full of gooey cheese.
She whimpered in a quiet voice,
"I need some water, please."

The friends all looked at Lola
Not believing their own eyes,
For her tiny mousey tummy
Had grown to twice its size.

Because they all loved Lola
They forgave her for her greed.
"God would do the same," they said
And helped their friend in need.

As she lay there on the floor
Lola finally understood
That keeping all things for herself
Just wasn't very good.

With cheesy breath, she blurted out,
"I'm sorry I didn't share.
Thank you for being such good friends
And showing that you care."

So now when treats and toys come out
Lola doesn't need her way.
"It's mine to share. It's yours and ours"
Is her favorite thing to say.

Do not forget to do good and to share with others.
Hebrews 13:16 NIV

Say NO to WHINING

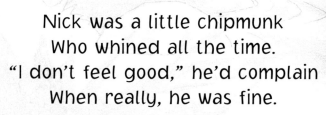

Nick was a little chipmunk
Who whined all the time.
"I don't feel good," he'd complain
When really, he was fine.

Nick whined in a high-pitched voice
And sometimes shed some tears.
His friends would roll their eyes
And put their paws over their ears.

Nick's whining and complaining
Would have gone on like that
If his little sister, Tiny,
Had not become a copycat.

When their mother called,
"Kids, come on in!"
"Kids, come on in!"
Tiny copied with a grin.

"I'm tired and my toes hurt,"
Nick whined, rubbing his paw.
Tiny looked at her brother
And said, "Blah, blah, blah, blah, blah."

"That's not what I said,
If you're trying to copy me."
Nick glared at his sister
As mad as he could be.

"When you whine," Tiny said,
"'Blah, blah, blah' is all I hear.
Just 'blah, blah, blah, blah, blah,'
Going into my ear."

"But I'm bored and I'm hungry!
That's what I say all the time!"
But when Nick said that to Tiny
It did sound like a whine.

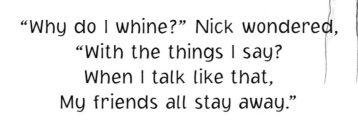

"Why do I whine?" Nick wondered,
"With the things I say?
When I talk like that,
My friends all stay away."

"God tells us to be joyful
And not complain or groan.
I'll ask my friends for help
And learn to use a happy tone."

Tiny walked right up to Nick.
"Blah, blah, blah," she teased.
Then Nick said, "No more blah, blah, blah,"
And he felt very pleased.

Now when Nick feels like whining,
He knows he has a choice.
Instead he laughs and jokes
And speaks in a happy voice.

Do everything without complaining or arguing.
Philippians 2:14 NIV

Say Yes to RESPECT

Rex just loved the great big circus.
His favorites were the raccoon clowns;
Their juggling act always made him laugh.
Hooray! The circus was coming to town!

"Set the table, Rex," Mom called.
"Time for dinner, everyone."
"You're not the boss of me!" Rex yelled.
"I'll do it when I'm done."

God tells us in the Bible
How we should treat each other:
Show respect to old and young,
And honor your father and mother.

Three rings and a flying trapeze,
Huge tents reached toward the sun.
"Let's go!" Rex called to Sophie and Sam.
"This will be so fun!"

Once inside the great big tent,
Rex ran down to the front.
"Please move back," the ringmaster said.
"I'm afraid you might get bumped."

"You're not the boss of me!"
Rex rudely yelled to the ringmaster.
And that bad show of disrespect
Led to a huge disaster!

A raccoon clown came dancing by
And bumped Rex, who tumbled down.
Rex called, "Hey, be more careful!"
"You're not my boss," snapped the clown.

"That clown is very rude!" Rex thought.
"What an ugly thing to say.
He should treat me with respect.
Why would someone act that way?"

As Rex sat there on the floor,
More clowns came by with a dancing bear.
The entire group tripped over Rex;
Juggling balls flew in the air.

One ball hit the lion's nose:
He let out a big, loud roar.
The elephant stomped at the noise.
The balancing skunks fell to the floor.

The skunks hit the mouse who was selling snacks;
Cotton candy flew into the air
Then came back down, spilling out,
And stuck in Rex's hair!

"We could have avoided this mess," Rex moaned.
"The circus wouldn't be wrecked.
If only I had listened to God
And treated others with respect!"

Show proper respect to everyone.
1 Peter 2:17 NIrV

Say Yes to CLEAN-UP

Sophie asked her good friend Lucy,
"Do you want to make a treat?"
"Why yes," she said. "I'm hungry.
Let's make something sweet."

Sophie loved making pudding;
Chocolate was the best.
She knew Mom's rule: use what you need,
And clean up all the mess.

Measuring, pouring, mixing—
The girls had so much fun.
Sugar here, chocolate there,
What a mess when they were done!

When Sophie ran outside to play
Lucy followed, running faster.
The girls forgot Mom's clean-up rule
And, oh, what a disaster!

Drops of milk dripping down,
Sugar smashed into the floor.
Dirty bowls and measuring cups,
Chocolate handprints on the door.

The kitchen was suddenly quiet.
Then came the perfect chance
For little creatures to march on in—
Teeny, tiny armies of ants!

Through the chocolate, through the sugar,
Ants and ants galore
Marching, marching, on the counter,
More and more and more.

"Let's go eat the pudding,"
Lucy called as they ran back.
But as they reached the kitchen
They found the pudding under attack.

Ants were crawling everywhere;
The girls stared at the sticky mess.
Then Lucy jumped and wiggled and kicked;
The ants were crawling up her dress!

She jumped around as she cried out,
"We can't eat chocolate pudding with ants.
I wish we'd obeyed your Mom and cleaned up
When we had the chance."

Sophie and Lucy scrubbed and cleaned;
They washed away the ant parade.
And then they had to throw away
The pudding they had made.

It's OK to make a mess;
In fact, it's rather fun.
Just remember to listen to Mom
And clean up when you're done!

My child, obey the teachings of your parents.
Proverbs 1:8 CEV

Say NO to MEANiES

Sophie skipped out to the mailbox
To check if there was mail.
But when she reached in for the letters
She saw a long, gray tail.

For hiding behind the magazines
And a package that was there
Was Sophie's brother, Sam,
With a stamp stuck in his hair.

"Why are you hiding?
You should come out and play."
"I'm sad because the meany boys
Laughed at me today."

"Sam, you should go talk with them
And tell them what you think."
"I think they hurt my feelings.
Being laughed at really stinks!"

Later on that day,
Sophie thought she'd get a treat.
But when she looked inside the cupboard
She saw cheesy snacks and two gray feet.

"Sam, you must stop hiding
In the mail and tortellinis.
Go talk with that group of boys
Who are such teasing meanies!"

The next day, on the way to school,
Sam saw those meany mice.
He knew just how he'd tell them
That their teasing was not nice.

"It's wrong to tease and say mean things.
God says what we should do:
'Be kind and treat each other
How you'd want them to treat you.'"

But when he walked up to the meanies
Sam found to his surprise
That the meany boys were being teased
By some boys twice their size.

The big boys laughed and ran away,
And the meanies began to cry.
At first Sam didn't want to help
But then decided he would try.

The meanies all were so surprised
When Sam helped them from their knees.
"I'm sorry they hurt your feelings.
It doesn't feel good to be teased."

"You're right," the meany boys said.
"Being laughed at isn't fun.
So let's be friends instead.
Our teasing days are done!"

**If your brother sins against you,
go and tell him what he did wrong.
Matthew 18:15 ICB**

Say Yes to FOLLOWING the RULES

Deep in the woods lived Jack the raccoon,
Who ran from every rule.
He got in trouble all the time
And thought he was so cool.

Jack had a very best friend named Sam,
Who loved to come and play.
But because Jack broke the rules a lot
He was in time-out most of the day.

Jack decided to run away;
With Sam, he snuck out the door.
Together they talked about what to do;
They would follow rules no more!

"I will eat cake for breakfast," Jack laughed.
"And I'll only watch cartoons.
I'll snack on candy all day long
And never clean my room!"

As the boys were making plans
They kept walking through the woods.
Soon they saw a river
And looked down from where they stood.

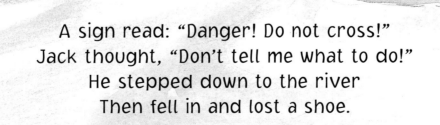

A sign read: "Danger! Do not cross!"
Jack thought, "Don't tell me what to do!"
He stepped down to the river
Then fell in and lost a shoe.

Jack's foot shot up as he yelled out,
"A crab has grabbed my toe!"
Jack's face turned red; his eyes grew big.
"Oh, please, just let it go!"

The crab pinched hard and stayed on tight.
Jack looked like he could cry.
While Jack then shook his foot around,
The crab stared him in the eye.

The crab said in his crabby voice,
"I vill not let you be!
For you deed not obey that sign
And almost smooshed my family!"

Finally the crab loosened his grip.
"Raccoon, you must vatch out.
Rules keep us safe and happy;
That's vhat they're all about."

Jack climbed out and limped back home;
His foot was oh so sore.
"I don't want to hurt anyone.
I'll run from rules no more!"

Remember, God gave you a mom, a dad,
Or maybe a crabby creature
To help you learn to follow rules,
Keep you safe, and be your teacher.

**Follow my rules. Be careful to obey my laws.
Then you will live safely in the land.
Leviticus 25:18 NIrV**

Say Yes to MANNERS

In the woods where the animals lived
Was a secret tree house hideaway.
Before you could get in this fort
There were special words you had to say.

The secret code had just one rule.
Good manners were what it was all about.
If you were mean or rude or selfish,
Then you simply had to stay out!

Wilbur, a rude little porcupine,
Wanted to go to the big tree house.
So he waddled to find his good friend Sam;
Off they went, porcupine and mouse.

They both were so excited
At the secret hideaway.
"Please, may I come in?" Sam asked.
The door flew open. "Yes, you may!"

Then in a rather sassy voice,
Wilbur said, "Let me in too!"
The door closed shut and Wilbur frowned,
Not sure what he should do.

Then Wilbur saw a long, green vine;
He jumped up and grabbed on tight.
He swung on it like a monkey would
And kicked with all his might.

The door just wouldn't open;
Wilbur fell on his behind.
"Why can't I get inside this place?
It's just not fair!" he whined.

Wilbur's friends Lucy and Liv
Came to the fort to play.
"Please, may we come in?" they asked.
The door swung wide. "OK!"

Wilbur thought, "May I come in?
Isn't that what I said before?
So how come when I say it out loud
It doesn't open the secret door?"

Then suddenly he remembered
All the times that he had heard
His mom ask him the question,
"What's the magic word?"

Wilbur ran up to the door
He knew exactly what to do
"Please, may I come in?" he asked.
The door opened up. "Thank you!"

Being polite is important;
It's easy to say "thanks" and "please."
God wants us to use good manners
And say kind words like these!

Always be humble and gentle.
Patiently put up with each other and love each other.
Ephesians 4:2 CEV

Say NO to ARGUING

Bits and Cole were two little twins—
One a sister, one a brother.
They should have been the best of friends
But always argued with each other.

"Hey! Your foot is touching mine,
So move it!" Bits would say.
Then Cole would tease, "Too bad, twin sis!
I want my foot to stay!"

Here's the funny thing, my friends,
About these two silly twins—
Even though they always argued
No one would ever win!

They argued when they brushed their teeth.
They argued when they combed their hair.
They argued when they rode their bikes.
They argued almost everywhere.

They argued in front of their mom.
They argued in front of their dad.
They argued in front of Sophie and Sam.
They always sounded mad.

One day when Bits and Cole went out
With several friends to play,
Bits had a very red, sore throat
And could not talk that day.

Cole started poking at Bits;
To her tail he gave a tweak.
Bits opened her mouth to argue;
All that came out was a squeak.

"What happens now?" they wondered.
"I guess we can't argue today.
Instead of sitting here fighting
Let's join our friends and play."

So the twins spent no time arguing;
They just played in the park.
Then one by one, the friends went home
'Cause it was getting dark.

When Cole and Bits stopped playing,
They saw the day was done.
Their friends were gone; the sun was down;
The twins had had such fun!

"I think we miss out on a lot
When we argue with each other.
Let's learn to work it out because
God says, 'Love one another.'"

Now if one tries to start a fight
And argue when they speak,
To stop the fight before it starts
The other just yells, "Squeak!"

**The Lord's servant must not quarrel;
instead, he must be kind to everyone.
2 Timothy 2:24 NIV**

Say Yes to THANKiNG GOD

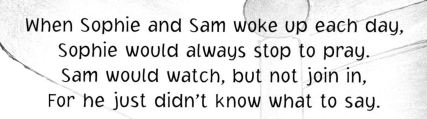

When Sophie and Sam woke up each day,
Sophie would always stop to pray.
Sam would watch, but not join in,
For he just didn't know what to say.

"Just talk to God like He's your friend;
Thank Him for making a sunny day.
It's easy to say 'Thanks!'" Sophie said,
"For family and friends and time to play."

Sophie always remembered to say grace
At every meal, before she ate.
"I'd like to do that, too," Sam said,
"But it wouldn't sound so great."

"Thank God for your favorite foods,
For all the yummy things you eat,
Like peanut butter and jelly beans,
Pizza or an ice cream treat."

One day – *Crash!* The thunder boomed!
Sam was scared of the loud, dark storm
But Sophie, like always, stopped to pray,
"God, please keep us safe and warm."

"How can you pray when you're afraid?"
Sam asked, with his eyes open wide.
"'Cause God wants us to talk to Him,
Especially when we're scared inside."

At night when they were tired
And it was time to go to bed
Sophie said her goodnight prayers
While Sam just bowed his head.

"Sam, God wants to hear from you—
Talking to God would make Him so glad.
Tell Him thanks for someone you love
Like Nick and Tiny, or Mom and Dad."

"Don't just talk, but listen, too,
And let me tell you the very best part:
When you stop to listen to God
You hear Him answer in your heart."

The next morning when the day began,
Sophie woke up and heard something new—
There by his bed, Sam was praying,
"Dear God, I'd like to talk to You...

"Thank You for my fire truck,
For slimy worms and bumblebees.
Thanks for that huge muddy puddle.
I'm glad You healed my skinned-up knees."

"I'm sorry when I get in trouble—
Help me be better and try again.
Thank You for my best friend, Jack.
It's fun to talk to You...AMEN!"

Spend a lot of time in prayer. Always be watchful and thankful.
Colossians 4:2, NIrV